For our parents —S.L. and M.L.

Text copyright © 2018 by Suzanne Lang
Jacket art and interior illustrations copyright © 2018 by Max Lang

All rights reserved. Published in the United States by Random House Children's Books,
a division of Penguin Random House LLC, New York.

Random House and the colophon are registered trademarks of Penguin Random House LLC.

Visit us on the Web! rhcbooks.com

Educators and librarians, for a variety of teaching tools, visit us at RHTeachersLibrarians.com

Library of Congress Cataloging-in-Publication Data is available upon request.
ISBN 978-0-553-53786-4 (trade) — ISBN 978-0-553-53787-1 (lib. bdg.) —
ISBN 978-0-553-53788-8 (ebook)

MANUFACTURED IN CHINA
22
First Edition

GRUMPY MONKEY

By Suzanne Lang

Illustrated by Max Lang

Random House 🏠 New York

One wonderful day Jim Panzee woke to discover that nothing was right.

The sun was too bright, the sky was too blue, and the bananas were too sweet.

Jim was confused.

"What's going on?"

"Maybe you're grumpy," suggested
Norman from next door.

"I'm not grumpy!" Jim insisted.

On his walk he met Marabou.

"Jim's grumpy," Norman told Marabou.

"Why are you grumpy, Jim?" asked Marabou.

"It's such a wonderful day."

"Grumpy! Me? I'm not grumpy," said Jim.

"But look at how you're standing," Marabou said.

"It's true," said Norman. "You're all hunched."

So Jim loosened up.

Then he ran into Lemur.

"Jim's grumpy," Norman told Lemur.

"Why are you grumpy, Jim?" asked Lemur.

"It's such a wonderful day."

"Grumpy! Me? I'm not grumpy," said Jim.

"Your eyebrows look grumpy,"
said Lemur.

"It's true," said Norman. "They're
all bunched up."

So Jim raised his brow.

Then he tripped over Snake.

"Oh no," said Norman. "That's the last thing you need when you're feeling so grumpy."

"Grumpy! Me? I'm not grumpy," said Jim.

"Then why that frown?" said Snake.

"I think it's because he tripped over you,"
Norman whispered to Snake.

So Jim put on a smile.

Finally Jim looked happy.

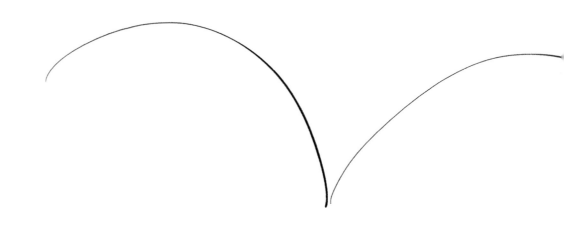

But he didn't feel happy inside.

Everyone wanted Jim to enjoy this wonderful day.
"You should sing with us!" said the birds.

Jim didn't feel like singing.

"You should swing with us!"
said the monkeys.
Jim didn't feel like swinging.

"You should roll with us!" said the zebras.
Jim didn't feel like rolling.

"You should stroll with us!" said the peacocks.
Jim didn't feel like strolling.

"You should lie in the grass!"

"You should stomp your feet!"

"You should take a bath!"

"And make a splash!"

"You should hug someone!"

"You should laugh!"

"You should take a nap!"

"You should eat old meat!"

"Or some honey!"

"You should jump
up and down!"

"You should sit in the sun!"

"You should dance!"

But Jim didn't feel like doing any of that.

"Why are you grumpy, Jim?" asked the others. "It's such a wonderful day."

shouted Jim as he beat his chest.

And he stormed off.

Jim felt sorry. A little sorry for shouting at
everyone but mostly sorry for himself.
"I guess I am grumpy," Jim sighed.
And just as he was starting to feel really sad . . .

. . . he came upon Norman. Norman was slumped. His eyebrows were bunched up, and he was frowning.

"What's the matter? Are you grumpy?" asked Jim.

"No. I danced with Porcupine," said Norman.

"Are you okay?" asked Jim.

"It hurts, but I'll probably feel better soon enough," said Norman. "Are you still grumpy?"

"Yes," said Jim, "but *I'll* probably feel better soon enough, too. For now, I need to be grumpy."

"It's a wonderful day to be grumpy," said Norman.

Jim agreed.

And he already felt a little bit better.